READERS LOVE BOOKS BY JACKIE KESWICK

JOB HUNT

Job Hunt is a very well-written, fast-paced, action-packed, thrilling piece of entertainment that kept me glued to the pages. — Prism Book Alliance

This book was fun to read and damn hot. Just reading it set my sheets on fire. — MM Good Book Reviews

GHOSTS

...a mellower, slightly introspective read with a beauty all of its own. — Boy Meets Boy Book Reviews

This book was a different kind of wonderful than the first, quieter, slower, more down to earth and less cyberspace-high. I read it with a wistful smile and closed it with a happy sigh. — Prism Book Alliance

HOUSE HUNT

This next part of Jack's journey to finding a man to love and a real home remains thriller-level exciting, emotionally engaging, and has more twists and turns than I thought possible. — Rainbow Book Reviews

House Hunt is another double thriller from Jackie Keswick. It's suspenseful, fast paced and action packed, and keeps you on the edge of your seat. — The Novel Approach

Contemporary Romance from Jackie Keswick

Zero Rising

The Power of Zero ✦ Two Divided by Zero ✦ Zero Tolerance

The Power of Zero

Job Hunt ✦ Ghosts ✦ House Hunt ✦ Swings & Roundabouts
✦ Dating Games

Dwight & Conrad Casefiles

Mouse Hunt ✦ A Very Winston Christmas ✦ Grand Union
Hunt ✦ When the Law Needs Help

White Knight Security

A Knight to Remember ✦ Grant ✦ Rylan ✦ Luca ✦ Fritz ✦
Christmas Knights

Rock & Art Theft

Undercover Star ✦ Here for You ✦ Sanctuary Found

Standalone Stories

Leap of Faith ✦ Crossfire ✦ Baubles ✦ Cosy & Chill ✦ A Box
of Wishes ✦ Hiding Place ✦ Promised before Wind and Tide

WHITE KNIGHT SECURITY

JACKIE KESWICK

CHAPTER ONE

"Not another babysitting job!" Grant threw himself into a chair and tossed his leather jacket onto another. Heaven knew why he'd brought it with him. The early summer heatwave made it unnecessary.

"Stop whining. You suggested we offer bodyguard services, remember?"

Grant sighed. "Cap … I know they're valuable jobs, and worthwhile ones, too, but this is the sixth in a row. I'm so bored I'm losing the will to live."

"Are you now?" Fritz's expression didn't change as he pushed a folder across the desk. "Here. Got an email enquiry yesterday morning. Prelims make my nose itch. He's coming in at nine for a chat. Listen in. If you really don't want this one, ask Luca to take it. You're the only two with room in your schedules this week."

That should please him, Grant knew. When they'd set up White Knight Security after leaving the army,

Grant had worried work might be too thin on the ground to keep the four of them fed. Rescuing Amelie Croft two days before Christmas had brought their nascent business a grant from the LightSpiel Foundation, Amelie's expertise in setting up the legal and financial side of White Knight Security, and recommendations to her and her husband's friends and clients. On top of that, they'd had Fritz's power of persuasion. Fritz—whose aunt had lived in the area for generations and had known absolutely everyone—had worked through Isabel Knight's huge list of contacts, offered help and asked for referrals. Half a dozen small jobs later, they'd been up and running, and their firm grew busier by the week. They offered private investigations, surveillance, and close protection. They'd even done a couple of jobs in tandem with the local police force. Grant loved it, but he preferred to be up and doing. Close protection, where he needed to stick to his target like glue even if they spent their day in an office, was his least favourite job.

"What is it this time?" He opened the folder, and his jaw dropped when he saw the photo on the first page. "Fuck me!"

The image showed a man leaning against a railing. The grin on his face—half sultry, half mischievous—

tightened every muscle in Grant's body. He was a sucker for dark eyes and golden hair. So what?

"Stunning, right? He's a trauma surgeon at Stoke Mandeville. Excellent credentials."

"And he needs us because?"

"He has a stalker."

Grant's gaze was glued to the photo. He sensed the focus and dedication behind the cheeky grin, and he didn't want to imagine fear on those enticing features. "Why doesn't he go to the police?"

"Precisely what I'm going to ask him," Fritz replied. "Are you in, or shall I talk to Luca?"

"No. I'm in." Grant's voice came out scratchy and rough. When was the last time he'd reacted like this to a mere photo? *Fucking never.* He closed the folder and stood. Cold water. That was what he needed. Cold water, and then coffee and half a dozen Danish pastries. "I'll get set up next door."

"You do that." Fritz didn't look up. Grant imagined he was smirking. And wasn't that annoying?

Spencer found the offices of White Knight Security in a tiny village halfway between London and Oxford.

From an arched gate, the drive led to a square-set manor house built from brick and timber. It stood on the edge of a lake, which Spencer hadn't spotted through the thick stand of ash and beech trees shielding the house from the road. He wondered whether it had started life as a moat.

A peaceful place to work, and an even better place to live. Spencer imagined himself sitting at the end of the short jetty, glass of wine in hand and feet dangling in the water, watching the sunset without a care in the world.

Dreams and make-believe, of course. Worries were omnipresent, even for people who owned a gorgeous house beside a lake.

He turned off his engine and checked his watch.

Fifteen minutes early. Damn! His mind was uneasy enough without spare time to second-guess his decision to consult a security company. He needed to move. Stretch his legs. Walk to the lake or up the drive to admire the house.

A knock on his side window made him jump. Damn, he was nervous! He got out of the car. "Sorry. You startled me."

"Dr Corel?"

"Yes. No. Mister, please. I'm a surgeon. And I ... I'm

early."

"Not a problem. I'm Fritz Bronnley."

"Oh." Spencer had made an appointment with the head of a private security firm, not a man who looked like an investment banker. Fritz Bronnley's deep blue silk shirt brought out the touch of silver in his dark hair, and his relaxed demeanour suggested that the day's biggest challenge was his golf handicap.

"Would you like to come inside?" Bronnley offered a reassuring smile. "We have coffee."

"Oh yes, please. You'd be saving my life."

"Really now?"

"Night shift," Spencer explained. "An uneventful one—which I normally don't complain about. Only…"

"It leaves you too much time to think."

Now here's a man with an excellent bedside manner. Spencer followed Bronnley into the house. Maybe this wouldn't be as embarrassing as the police interview had been. The aroma of freshly brewed coffee calmed him further, as did the murmur of conversation from somewhere nearby.

"How do you like your caffeine?"

"Black with three sugars." Spencer grinned at the startled once-over Bronnley bestowed on him. He was too thin and knew it. "I have a hectic job."

"Obviously." Bronnley took his coffee black with no adornment. "If you'd like to come this way?"

In his office, Bronnley bypassed the desk and made a beeline for the walnut and cream leather sofa by the French doors.

"That's a lovely view."

"Seconded. I sit here for hours and dream of fishing."

"Right." First impressions aside, Spencer couldn't see Bronnley sitting and daydreaming. Be up and organising, yes. Though he appreciated how neatly Bronnley had settled his unease. And the man's choice in sofas was flawless.

Spencer sank into the soft leather and sighed. This mess with Carlo exhausted him more than a double shift in the A&E department. He took a sip of coffee and let his gaze roam the water. Bronnley waited for the caffeine to do its work, and Spencer appreciated that, too.

"Thank you for giving me the chance to collect myself."

"No need to thank me. We're prepared for tough conversations."

"And used to them?"

"Certainly. Our clients come to us because they have a problem they cannot handle alone. We have the specialist skills they need, but that doesn't mean they feel comfortable asking. Much like your work, no?"

"That's an excellent analogy." Spencer relaxed a touch more. He'd worried about appearing helpless, but Bronnley had nipped that idea in the bud. "Definitely not like taking my car for repair. There, at least, I have a vague idea how it's done, even if I don't want to do it myself." He took another sip of coffee and squared his shoulders. "What is your intake process? Do I talk or do you ask questions?"

"Could you start by summarising the problem for me? Then I'll ask questions to tease out details."

Spencer clutched his mug, letting the last of the warmth seep into his hands. "I'm a trauma surgeon, working mainly at Stoke Mandeville, though I fill in elsewhere if I'm needed. And for the last… maybe eight weeks… someone's been following me."

Bronnley raised a hand, and Spencer paused.

"Why the qualifier? You said *maybe* eight weeks?"

"That's when I began to notice it. Doesn't mean that's when it started. At first, I wasn't sure it was real. I'd been working long shifts and thought it was just exhaustion. Then I found my letterbox vandalised.

Filled with paint. Someone broke into my office at the hospital. I received… bizarre gifts. A car swerved and almost hit me as I was shopping in Aylesbury. And now I can't shake this crawling sensation, as if someone's watching me. Even when I'm operating." Spencer's hands trembled, and he set the mug down.

This is why you're here, he told himself. *Because you can't have it affect your work.* He met Bronnley's eyes. "Individually, none of these things are significant. But one after the other, and over weeks—"

"An excess of coincidences. Has something like this happened to you before?"

"No."

"And you think you know the culprit?"

"I thought it was my ex, but the facts don't fit. Not all of them." Spencer felt himself grow agitated once more.

"Nasty breakup?" Bronnley asked, reading between the lines. "How long were you in a relationship?"

"Nine months, and I should have left him sooner." Bronnley didn't blink at the pronoun, and Spencer's opinion of the man's bedside manner rose another notch.

"He was violent?"

"Not physically, not yet. Controlling, undermining,

and eventually verbally abusive. Interspersed with the usual apologies, declarations of affection, and promises to mend his behaviour."

"Which you recognised and didn't fall for."

"I gave him the benefit of the doubt for longer than I probably should have."

"But it's difficult to deceive a professional who recognises the patterns, right? Tell me which of the events you attributed to him. What's his name, by the way?"

"Carlo Sigismund. He's a stockbroker with an office in High Wycombe. I thought he was sending the flowers, and that he was following me when I was driving home after work."

"What doesn't fit?"

"He has no reason to break into my office or wreck my letterbox. I can't see him hanging around in the hospital to spy on me—he has a busy job of his own. If he wanted us back together, why would he try to run me over? And why wait for seven months before making the attempt, anyway?"

"Quite," Bronnley said, not an ounce of judgement in his tone. "You said you went to the police. How did that go?"

"As if I was a hysterical twelve-year-old afraid of

clowns. Maybe I shouldn't have mentioned feeling watched. Or reported it closer to home instead of going to High Wycombe."

"Why did you? Because you thought Carlo Sigismund was involved?"

"Partly, yes. But also … I was there, if that makes sense. I walked past the police station and suddenly thought I should make a report. It was stupid."

"I disagree with you there. Tell me what they said."

"The most likely culprits for the vandalised letterbox were bored kids. A cleaner who'd lost their keys could have broken into my office."

"Why a cleaner?"

Spencer shrugged. "Because nothing was stolen? Did I mention that?"

"What about the car that tried to hit you? Did they offer a clever explanation for that?"

"Of course. It was a swerve my mind amplified into danger. The officer I spoke to was kind enough to suggest I take a holiday." Spencer wrapped his arms around himself, not caring it signalled how upset he was. He was here to hire private security precisely *because* he couldn't cope with the situation. "The police prefer the reports from a reputable businessman with a reasonable story to the ravings of a high-strung, overworked doctor." The words tasted bitter. Spencer said them anyway. "Carlo has friends in the police."

Bronnley's smile held a tiny, feral edge. "So do we, Mr Corel. So do we."

CHAPTER TWO

Grant didn't appreciate an audience while he packed. He hated it even more when the audience was as full of snarky comments as Luca Birch.

"You're so screwed. That doctor is yummy. Like honey and chocolate rolled into one. So totally your type."

"Shut up." The words lacked heat. They'd known each other for years and hadn't hidden their bedroom preferences from each other. Not once they discovered they batted for the same team. Like Grant, Luca liked his men long and lean, but there, the similarities ended. Grant had a thing for dark-eyed blonds—and their new client ticked that box with abandon.

"Any thoughts on the stalker?" he asked to forestall more comments designed to rile him.

"I'd put money on the ex, though the police

response bothers me. Stalkers are nasty, man. They escalate. And the doctor doesn't strike me as someone crying wolf."

"No, he doesn't." Spencer Corel had shown signs of nerves, but those hadn't lasted past the first few minutes. Then he'd been coherent, concise, and not a little vexed. He hadn't portrayed himself as a victim, nor someone seeking attention. Grant knew what *that* looked like. He even had the scars to prove it.

"I read him as someone coming to us because he's aware he's out of his depth. Check with the police? If they had a proper reason to blow him off, we need to know." Grant zipped his bag and slung it over his shoulder. "I'll dig into the ex. It'd be easier to ask questions while I'm watching over the doc. I'll ask around in the hospital, too. Someone must have seen something. Especially about that break-in."

"And those gifts. I got the impression he wasn't just talking about flowers."

"Yes, those too." Grant threw a last look around his tidy bedroom. "Let's go meet the client. I'm sure Fritz has finished reading him the playbook."

"Look at you, all eager and shit," Luca grinned. "I hope you've packed a leash."

"Arsehole." The insult was half-hearted, because

Grant *was* eager to meet Spencer Corel. Most of his close protection clients to date had been businessmen. Corporate types, who spent their days behind a desk. Corel Spencer's workplace was an operating theatre and instead of shuffling money, he saved people's lives. Watching over Spencer wouldn't be boring.

Spencer drove through tiny lanes, following the directions from his GPS and checking every now and then that Grant's truck was still behind him. He'd explored the Chiltern Hills on foot and by bike since moving here four years ago. How had he missed such a scenic area?

Could he have spotted Grant Keeping in a restaurant or bar in Amersham or High Wycombe? Or met him in the pub of one of the many villages? Grant's ocean-blue eyes with their long dark lashes would have stopped Spencer in his tracks. He had liked Grant's hands, too. Broad, with strong fingers, they'd felt dependable, even though they'd exchanged nothing more than a polite handshake.

And Grant hadn't pitied him.

None of the men at White Knight Security had.

They'd listened to his story and had made plans to verify each incident, find witnesses and interview bystanders. They were going to run down the stalker, while Grant ensured Spencer was neither molested nor disturbed while he worked.

Why can't you sort out your own mess? You're supposed to be the clever one here. The whispers of his subconscious mind sounded suspiciously like Carlo.

"Fuck you!" Spencer snarled and dug in the console for a chocolate bar. He didn't regret his decision to hire White Knight Security, and his inner critic could fuck right off. Besides, he had a house guest to look after and wondering about dinner was more productive than arguing with Carlo's ghost.

Spencer took a mental inventory of his fridge and larder. He wasn't an accomplished chef, but he liked to putter around the kitchen, especially when he wasn't just cooking for himself. He decided on grilled salmon, green beans, and coconut rice for dinner, and turned off the road on a detour to pick up an after-dinner treat.

Grant was quick to notice, appearing beside Spencer before he'd even left his car.

"Why are you stopping? This isn't Aston Clinton."

"I remembered I have nothing sweet at home. And

this," Spencer waved at the colourful storefront, "is one of my favourite bakeries."

"You want cake for lunch?"

Spencer checked his watch. Dinnertime was ages away. "Um … I think I misplaced a few hours. Happens sometimes after a few night shifts. That said, I can eat cakes and biscuits at any hour. Do you have a favourite?"

"Do I have a favourite cake?"

"Yes. Do you?"

Grant stared at the bakery as if he faced a life-and-death decision. "From this place? Lemon meringue pie or Hazelnut Heaven," he said. "The triple chocolate and salted caramel is good, too. I also love anything with cinnamon and apples. And—" The grin lighting his face made Spencer's knees wobble. "I can eat cake at any hour, too."

A sleeping Spencer Corel was the cutest thing. He lay on his side, one hand tucked under his cheek, and hadn't moved a muscle for two hours.

Watching Spencer sleep was both soothing and humbling. Spencer trusted Grant, a total stranger, not to hurt him. The way he'd given Grant the run of the house had been equally casual.

In Grant's line of work, that was rare. Most of their clients resented needing protection. They hated him prying into their affairs, never realising that lying and withholding information put their own and their guard's lives in danger.

Boredom wasn't the only reason Grant disliked close protection jobs. The disdain and unconcern many clients treated him with played a large part, too. Maybe now White Knight Security had plenty of work coming in, they could focus on clients who appreciated their help.

His phone buzzed. Grant retreated into the kitchen to avoid waking the sleeping man.

"Hey," he answered.

"Why are you whispering?"

"Doc's asleep. He had night shifts, yes? Don't want to wake him."

"Whipped already? Luca said you were." Rylan's deep voice rang with amusement.

"You're a riot. Are you back?"

"Not yet. Just been checking in. Luca says the officer who heard the doc's complaint is the ex's half-brother. So no guesses why he dissed it."

"Shit."

"Yeah. But also stupid. I'm sure the Cap will raise a stink next time he plays golf with one of the bigwigs."

"Raise a stink? The Cap?"

"You know what I mean. Luca said they're going to re-open the complaint and investigate it properly."

"We can do it faster."

"Sure. We have your back, bro."

Rylan hung up, giving Grant no chance to thank him. But Grant *was* grateful. That their team was still together. That they'd stopped Fritz from selling Knightdale Court and had turned it into their home and business as intended. And that Spencer's story had one more leg to stand on.

It made for an easier life.

CHAPTER THREE

The green beans were done. The coconut rice was getting there. Spencer snagged a fourth champagne truffle from the open box and popped it into his mouth. The crisp chocolate shell cracked between his teeth, and he had to stop himself from moaning when the creamy filling caressed his tongue. Dinner was only minutes away, but freshly made chocolates were a temptation too far. It wouldn't be the first time that he'd demolished the entire box in one night.

Not today, though. Today he'd share dinner with Grant and enjoy deep dish cookies for dessert.

"Come on, you beauties." Spencer lifted the salmon fillets from their marinade and slid them under the grill, enjoying the sudden hit of lemon and ginger in the air.

"That smells wonderful."

The voice came from the kitchen door, where Grant leaned, watching him cook. Were all bodyguards this gorgeous, or had he drawn the lucky straw? "Dinner's ready in five."

"Right. Need help with anything?"

Far from feeling uncomfortable about having a stranger in his home, Spencer felt so relaxed, he was almost floating. Strange. Lack of sleep had never affected him this way. "Cutlery and wine glasses." He pointed. "Wine is in the fridge door."

Spencer plated their dinners. He enjoyed being part of a couple, loved the way two men shared space and work. It was the reason he hadn't ended things with Carlo as soon as he showed his true colours. Not that he and Grant were a couple, of course, but the dynamic was the same and Spencer let himself enjoy it.

He carried the plates into the living room, where Grant was pouring wine, and joined him at the table.

"You don't have to cook for me. You know that, right?" Grant held up his glass and let the sun sparkle in the pale liquid.

Spencer watched him. The slow, deliberate way in which Grant spun the wineglass was mesmerising. It snared his gaze as if by magic.

It slowed his thoughts, too.

"I enjoy cooking," he managed, when Grant raised an eyebrow in question. "I rarely get the chance to cook for two. Let me make the most of it."

"Then why aren't you enjoying your creation?"

"I … what?" Spencer tore his eyes from Grant and the spinning wineglass and blinked the swirling room to rights. In front of him, his plate of salmon, beans, and rice sat untouched. "Oh, I … got distracted." He picked up his cutlery, fumbling the knife.

"You're so busy taking care of me, you forgot yourself."

Spencer shrugged off the criticism. Taking care of people was his job, and he was happy to continue the caretaking at home. Especially for a house guest like Grant.

"And you told me you weren't a good cook, when this coconut rice is epic! In fact, the entire dinner is…"

Spencer swayed in his seat as the ringing in his ears drowned out Grant's praise. His vision wavered, blurred as if he was watching Grant through a rain-streaked window.

Unease trickled down his spine.

"Doc? Spencer! Are you okay?"

Grant's face came closer, spun in a few sickening

circles, and then settled.

"Doc, are you okay?"

"I feel…" He assessed his body's responses and alarm—the professional kind—sliced through him in a red-hot wave. It pushed the swirling fog aside for long enough to ask a question. "Do you feel sick? Dizzy? Drowsy?"

Grant shook his head. "Not at all. Why?"

"Because I think…" The next wave of dizziness swallowed the thoughts, replaced them with a bout of heaving nausea. Hands clamped over his mouth, Spencer battled through both, fought for clarity. "Poisoned," he managed. "I think I've been poisoned."

"Damn it!" Grant was out of his chair so fast he sent it flying. He pulled Spencer upright and shook him. "Talk to me, Doc!"

Spencer mumbled words that made no sense and struggled to keep his eyes open.

Which poison acted so quickly? And when had Spencer taken it when he'd been in Grant's sight since he'd left Knightdale Court?

"Stay awake, Doc! Come on, stay with me. I'll call

for an ambulance."

"Charcoal."

"You … what?" Then the word sank in. Activated charcoal. Of course. "Where do you keep it? Bathroom?" He settled Spencer onto the sofa and went to ransack the bathroom, returning to the living room with a glass of black sludge. "Doc! Wake up and drink this crap."

He didn't know how he managed it, but he got the vile stuff into Spencer.

Then it was hurry up and wait, making Spencer comfortable, watching over him, and hoping his condition wouldn't deteriorate.

"Call Cap," he told his phone, taking Spencer's pulse for the fifth time in as many minutes. Nothing had changed. Spencer's heart beat strong and steady, only a little slower than Grant expected. His breaths came deep and even, and he was a loose, sprawling weight as if he was sleeping.

"Bronnley."

"It's Grant, Cap. The doc's been poisoned. Drugged. I don't know."

"He what? How? Never mind that. I'll be over. Did you call an ambulance?"

"He asked for charcoal. He's sleeping. I'm keeping

an eye."

"Probably safer that way. If anything changes—"

"I'll take him to the hospital."

"Call me if you do."

"Roger that." Grant wanted to hit something. He checked Spencer's pulse instead. Nothing had changed. As far as he could tell, the man was asleep.

Spencer had acted strange as soon as they'd sat down to dinner. Grant recalled lengthy blank stares and delays responding to questions. Spencer had blinked more, too, as if his vision was blurry. Then he'd asked if Grant felt sick and dizzy.

Had Spencer suspected the food? But what had he eaten or drunk that Grant hadn't touched?

The answer was obvious the moment Grant entered the kitchen. An open box of chocolates sat on the counter, and four truffles were missing. The same box of chocolates Spencer had pulled from his letterbox when they'd come home. The one Grant had quizzed him about.

Grant didn't touch the box.

He didn't put a fist through the wall in frustration.

Instead, he poured a glass of water and returned to the living room to watch over Spencer Corel and wait for his captain.

Fritz arrived twenty minutes later, still dressed in workout clothes and trailing an aura of wrath like a shroud. "What happened? How's the doctor?"

"Sleeping. Come in. Water?" Grant poured a glass. Fritz had to be thirsty if he'd interrupted his workout.

Fritz took the glass, drained it in one and held it out for a refill. "Tell me everything."

"I fucked up," Grant said.

"I asked for details, not your opinion."

Grant ground his teeth. Fritz could be such a bastard when he put his mind to it! Fine. He'd deal.

"We stopped on the way here to buy treats." Grant pointed to the large paper bag on the far end of the counter. "A box of chocolates was in the doc's letterbox. He took a nap, and when he woke, he insisted on cooking dinner. And he scoffed chocolates while he did."

Remembering Spencer in the kitchen, enjoying the opportunity to cook for two, had Grant choking on his fury. "Can you believe I even asked him about the bloody things?"

"What did he say?"

"He's subscribed to a chocolate club. Gets two boxes a month." Grant retrieved the outer wrapping from the recycling bin. "Here. Chocolate club box, address label with chocolate club logo, postage label from the Royal Mail. It didn't occur to me to confiscate the chocolates."

A heavy hand landed on his shoulder. "None of us expected that. The incidents so far were nuisance-level and minor property damage. Do you think it's the stalker escalating?"

"Not because of anything we've done. The chocolates were posted before Spencer came to see us. They were in the letterbox before anyone saw me with Spencer."

"Hm. Tell me the rest."

Grant stared at the empty spots in the chocolate box. "You know, I thought I was a sugar whore, but he has me beat."

"I noticed that. How many chocolates did he have?"

"Four. He was happy while he cooked. Smiling. We sat down to dinner, and he acted … weirdly. Stared at objects, lost track of the conversation, didn't eat, didn't *realise* he wasn't eating. He asked me if I felt sick or dizzy. Then he told me he'd been poisoned."

"And then?"

"Got drowsy. I gave him a dose of charcoal and now he's sleeping. Pulse and breathing steady."

"Hopefully, he'll sleep off whatever it was. What a

shit fest!"

"I'm sorry, Cap. It's my—"

"Shut up. This is a step up from following the man or sending him flowers. This is GBH, if not attempted murder."

"If Spencer was right about the car trying to hit him, it's the second attempt."

"True." Fritz watched the sleeping man, then nodded to himself. "Stay with him, see how he goes. I'll get the chocolates analysed. Take him to the hospital if anything changes. And call for backup if you need it."

"Our schedules are—"

"Call for fucking backup! This is more serious than we expected, and we have your back. Understood?"

Grant touched his temple in a mini salute. "Understood."

The next day brought three car accidents, a burst appendix, and the usual fare of broken bones and unfortunate falls. Between one call and the next, finding time to use the bathroom became a challenge. Spencer gritted his teeth and dealt with case after case despite a throbbing head and a churning gut.

Suffering a massive hangover without the fun of a night out was unfair enough. That he now side-eyed every cup of coffee or plate of pastries someone handed him was worse.

At least Grant hadn't moved from his side. His unwavering presence warmed Spencer as much as finding him sitting on the floor by his bed this morning.

"That was my last case," he said when he left the operating room. "Time to head home."

Grant followed him. "They work you far too hard."

"You know it. If only people didn't get into cars."

"Or fell off ladders?"

"That too. In fact, I want people to stop hurting themselves and others. Period."

"Now, wouldn't that be nice? Though what would you do with yourself if you were no longer needed?"

"Oh, I don't know. Grow roses. Sit at the end of a pier and fish?" Spencer unlocked his office door and waved Grant inside.

"You've never really wondered about that, have you?"

"Nope. But I have wondered about what you're not telling me."

"Ah." For the first time, Grant didn't meet his gaze. "Didn't want to distract you from your work."

"I appreciate that, but I'm not working now."

"Cap called me earlier with news from the lab."

"The lab? You had the chocolates analysed?"

"Of course."

"I assume it was a tranquilliser?" A stray thought sent ice into his blood. "It wasn't Rohypnol, was it?"

Grant shook his head. "It was a low dose of Xylazine."

"What the fuck?" That was very nearly worse. "He laced the chocolates with animal tranqs?" His voice rose, and he didn't care. Carlo had tried to poison him, and it pissed him off.

"We're going to find out who sent them."

"Isn't it obvious?"

"No. The chocolates came by post and seeing them didn't surprise you."

"Because it's a subscription, I told you. I get a tasting box of chocolates every other week."

"Who knows about that?"

"Carlo, obviously."

"Did you live together?"

"No. But he stayed at my house as often as I stayed at his."

Grant considered that. "I'm not disbelieving you, just playing devil's advocate. I know he's top of your suspect list, but … this is a big step up from following you and sending you flowers. He'd have to order a box of chocolates. Unwrap them. Doctor them. Wrap them back up and post them again, making it look as if the sender hadn't changed."

"And your point is? He switches from actions that suggest he wants to resume the relationship to taking revenge for having been shown the door. That fits the pattern."

"What other gifts did you receive?"

Spencer felt himself blush and hated it. He was a grown man who didn't hide his inclinations. Talking to Grant shouldn't make a difference, even if he found him sexy.

"Doc?"

"Underwear, a leather harness, and sex toys," Spencer listed. To his relief, Grant's expression didn't change.

"Hence your question about the Rohypnol. Okay, I buy that. Next question is, do you want to report it to the police?"

"There's no point."

"It'd be different this time."

"I'm still cringing from the last time." Spencer sighed. "Sorry. I'm not usually so precious."

"You have every right to be. How are you feeling?"

"Truthfully? Like hammered shit."

That surprised a sputter out of Grant. "Don't give me that crap. You're tough as old boots."

"As long as you don't tell me I look like a pair."

"Don't fish. You're sexy and you know it."

Grant's grin did wonderful things to Spencer's insides. So did the roughened voice. "Do I?"

"You should." Grant turned his head away. "And I really shouldn't say such things."

"Why not?"

"It's unprofessional. You're a client."

"What if I wasn't a client?"

Grant didn't answer. And while Spencer hadn't expected him to, he now wished he hadn't asked.

"If you're still feeling off kilter … I make a mean chicken and ginger soup," Grant said as they headed home with Grant at the wheel of Spencer's car. Spencer could have driven himself, but Grant was feeling protective. He'd wanted Spencer to call in sick, but he'd lost that argument ten minutes after the man had woken.

Throughout the day, Spencer had acted as if nothing had occurred. Now he slumped in the passenger seat, eyes half shut, and dozed. Grant let him rest. He'd have plenty of time to ask questions once they were at the doc's house.

Grant drove through the villages to avoid the roadworks on the A41 and kept a close eye on the cars doing the same. The sudden bends and sharp dips took many by surprise.

"Watch for the wildlife!" The car in front almost hit a deer crossing the road, making Grant stomp on the brake.

His foot hit the floor of the car without resistance.

"What the fuck?"

He pumped the brake, fast and furious, then tried the pedal again.

Nothing.

"What is it?" Spencer sat up, as alert as he'd been that morning when the EMTs had piled into the A&E, crash victims on trolleys.

"No brakes." Grant shifted down, still working the brake pedal.

The road dipped and Spencer's car gathered speed,

catching up to slower traffic. The slope wasn't long, but it was steep, and Grant couldn't fucking overtake the slower cars with a lorry labouring up the hill in the opposite lane.

He leaned on the horn, shifted into third gear, and then into second. He swerved from side to side, using every inch of road, while cursing electronic parking brakes.

They barrelled down the steepest part of the hill, far too fast for the line of traffic. Then the truck in the opposite lane roared toward and past them. The passenger side front tyre hit a pothole, and the car flipped up and over.

Grant clutched the steering wheel. He heard Spencer swear and added choice words of his own. The car came down, upright again. Airbags burst around them, hemming them in and cushioning the landing.

Then it was quiet.

Too quiet?

The smell of burned rubber had Grant gagging, but he needed to move, talk, make sure that— "Doc?"

"Fine. Rattled. Mostly fine. You?"

"Pissed off. When did you have that car last serviced?"

"About a month ago? Are you sure you're not hurt? We landed hard on your side and—"

"I'm fine, Doc. Honestly." He dug for his phone as he spoke, and Spencer heard his sudden intake of breath.

"What?"

"Ribs. Where the seatbelt dug in. You'll have bruises, too, so don't fuss. I can handle bruises." He woke his phone and hit the speed dial. "I need backup," he barked.

"Where are you?"

"In a ditch on the road out of Flence Common. And I think this *was* the stalker escalating, in case you were wondering. The bloody brakes failed."

Chapter Four

Spencer hid in the shower under a stream of scalding water. It felt familiar. He'd weathered the worst days of his life with a succession of hot water, hot chocolate, cream horns, and triple chocolate and sea salt cookies.

Today, he felt especially battered, though his hurts were minor. When the car flipped, he'd regretted hiring White Knight Security and putting someone other than himself in danger.

That Grant had suffered nothing more serious than a collection of bruises and minor burns from the airbags didn't douse the guilt churning in his gut like spoiled food. His life was going off the rails, and he'd dragged a gorgeous man into the middle of the mess.

Wasn't it beyond unfair that the first man in months to catch his eye had to be someone he paid to look after him?

Emasculating, that's what it was. Or bad karma.

"Doc?" Grant poked his head around the bathroom door. "Don't turn into a prune. Come and eat something."

Facing Grant across a dinner table was the last thing Spencer wanted. But ignoring him wasn't polite, either. And once he stepped out of the steamy bathroom—dried and wearing his most comfortable clothes—he found that Grant's soup smelled so amazing, it made his mouth water.

"This is great," Spencer admitted fifteen minutes later, and held his bowl out for a refill.

"The comfort of chicken soup with a decidedly Asian kick." Grant topped up the doc's bowl, then added another ladleful to his own. He was relieved to see Spencer's mood improving. The accident had rattled him, but he had strategies lined up to help him cope. Seeing what Spencer did for a living, Grant supposed it made sense.

"I'm sorry," Spencer said. "I came to White Knight Security for help, not to put any of you in danger."

"I wasn't hurt."

"Bruises and burns don't qualify?"

"Not hugely, no. By the way … Your brakes didn't fail. Someone tampered with them."

"How did you learn that so quickly?"

"Cap called in a favour. A friend of his is an accident investigator. Getting his official report will take a few days, but that's his conclusion. And since the brakes were fine this morning, someone wrecked them in the hospital car park."

"Is it quick to do? Easy?"

"We'll ask Luca when we see him. He'll know."

Spencer's eyes crinkled as he smiled. "He has that sort of experience?"

"Luca's ace with cars. Also trucks, tractors, steamrollers, tanks … it moves, he can move it. Can you believe that he once grabbed us a combine harvester as transport? We thought he was taking the piss!"

"A combine harvester?"

"Cross my heart. He wanted the truck next to it, but that had a flat battery. So he took the harvester. I never appreciated how tall those buggers are, but the air-conditioned cab came in handy." Grant fished a hunk of chicken out of the soup and chewed. He'd been trying to cheer Spencer, but the memories came thick and fast now. It had been a beast of an op, and people he liked had died.

"Don't go there."

Spencer's fingertips brushed the back of his hand and stopped the swirling thoughts. "You read minds, now?"

"Just expressions. You're not the first veteran I've treated. Nor the first doctor who ever lost a patient."

"Oh. I didn't … I'd have said you're not used to violence."

"I deal with violence every bloody day. What do you think trauma surgery is, an old ladies' tea party?"

"You deal with the results of violence. The aftermath. You don't witness or inflict it. You certainly don't have it inflicted on you."

"So not my point."

"Then what is?"

Spencer took a deep breath. "You cooked me dinner and tried to cheer me up. Yet you were in that accident simply because I asked White Knight Security for help. You could have died in that wreck."

"So could you, but you're worried about *me* being hurt?"

"I don't want to see you hurt," Spencer muttered. "Is that so perplexing?"

Beet-red wasn't a colour that suited the doctor, but Grant found it as illuminating as Spencer's refusal to meet his gaze. "Not at all. More wine?"

"Morning, Grant! Breakfast will be just a minute. Help yourself to coffee." Spencer threw him a distracted smile and turned back to the stove.

Damn! Sleep-ruffled Spencer is sexy as fuck! Grant had slept little after their dinner conversation. Spencer's concern for his welfare had blended with the image of a bare-skinned, shadowed figure behind water-streaked glass to ruin his rest. And now here stood chocolate-eyed temptation in shorts and a T-shirt, offering coffee and breakfast.

Spencer Corel would be his ruin.

Grant was self-sufficient. He made his living keeping others safe. He didn't need looking after. But it was damned nice when it happened.

He drank his first coffee leaning against the window, pretending to watch the traffic passing Spencer's house.

The view across the kitchen was much more enjoyable, but Grant kept his gaze averted. Spencer was a client. Pinning him to the wall or bending him over the nearest table would be the height of unprofessional behaviour. Especially since they still had a stalker to find.

Luca's text had come at four that morning. He'd been the one following Carlo Sigismund, and he was adamant the man hadn't gone near the hospital or Spencer's car.

The only positive aspect of the previous days' attacks was more evidence to present to the police. And Luca's contact in the force had told him they were taking the threat seriously.

Grant wished they'd work faster.

He also wished they'd take their time, because spending his days with Spencer was becoming his goal in life.

"Eggs and bacon?" Spencer waved the spatula to attract his attention.

"Eggs and bacon," Grant agreed, caught in the intense gaze of Spencer's dark eyes.

Twenty minutes later, Grant wanted to run. Wanted to pound pavement until he lost himself in the exertion and stopped fantasising about Spencer. He couldn't go running, though. His place was in Spencer's home, watching Spencer's back.

He groaned. Yeah, that visual he could do without.

With running out of the question, he reached for a jump rope and headed out onto the deck.

The rhythmic slap of the rope soothed his agitation. He wasn't wearing headphones—he never did when he was on a job—but he imagined song after song from his playlist. He slowed and sped the rope to keep time, added twirls and crossovers, and fancy steps until nothing existed but the deck, the rope, and the beats in his mind.

When he resurfaced, muscles warm and loose, Spencer leaned against the wall, arms crossed. He'd watched Grant skipping and didn't hide that he liked what he saw. The bulge in his shorts was impressive, and the half-opened lips were an invitation.

Grant didn't stop to think. He crossed the deck until he was close enough to feel the heat from Spencer's body.

Spencer lifted his chin and met Grant's eyes. Then he wet his lips with the tip of his tongue.

The air caught fire, and Grant was done. He cupped Spencer's neck and hauled him across the few inches still separating them until he finally … finally! … got to taste the man.

From the first touch of lips to the moment he

wanted to rip Spencer's shorts off and bury himself in his arse, this wasn't a gentle kiss. This was hot and hungry, hard and grinding, and so damn good...

Grant staggered back, breath sawing in and out of his chest as if he'd run a race. He stared at Spencer, eyes dark, lips wet and bruised. And saw the surprise he felt stare back at him. Attraction, desire, raging lust—whatever this was, it had snared them both.

And that wasn't a good idea.

CHAPTER FIVE

For God's sake, stop thinking about that kiss! Grant wanted to tear something apart. He needed to be out and about, asking questions and rattling cages, not wondering why he'd broken off such an amazing kiss and left them both hanging. He also needed to be right here, guarding Spencer, and waiting for news from his teammates.

Talking of … He grabbed his phone and hit the speed dial.

"Let him sleep, for fuck's sake!" Rylan's deep rumble came from the speaker the moment the call connected.

"Morning to you, too."

"Hm."

"What is it? Are you okay? When did you get back?"

"Take a fucking number and stand in line."

Grant chuckled. "You must have come home looking rough. What happened?"

"Suicide attempt. Target drove his car into a fucking river!"

"Shit. Did you get him out?"

"Yeah. Police have him. Fritz found what the prosecution needed. Now shut up and let me ask the questions. I've been hearing all kinds of shit about you."

"Have you now?" The riled parts of Grant's mind finally settled. It sounded as if they'd kept their captain busy, and he'd come through for them as usual. And having Rylan back home meant he could breathe easier. He trusted Luca and Fritz with his life, but he and Rylan had been tight since basic training. That shit mattered.

"Cap said your doctor is under the cosh."

"Pretty much. Break-ins, unwanted gifts, poisoned chocolates, brakes tampered with. He thinks it's his ex, but I'm not sure. Not that I have a better idea."

"You like him." As always, Rylan's pronouncements came out of the blue and hit the bullseye.

"I like him."

"Bedded him yet?"

"He's a fucking client!"

"But you like him."

Grant ground his teeth. "He's totally my jam, as I'm sure Cap has told you. If he wasn't a client, I might have—" Oh fuck it! Just the thought of taking Spencer to bed sent heat into his belly. "Not gonna happen."

"Don't cut off your nose to spite your face."

"What does that even mean?"

Rylan chuckled. "I've never heard you sound so squirmy. It's … enlightening."

"I'm not going to fuck a client, however enlightening it is."

"He won't be a client forever. Don't nix the idea is what I'm saying, bro." He ended the call before Grant could argue. And wasn't that annoying?

Spencer felt antsy. He often did when he'd had a quiet afternoon, as if the lack of emergencies put him on edge. Grant's Range Rover was comfortable, but the passenger seat hugged him in an unfamiliar way and the haze of desire between them was thick enough to cut with a knife. They needed to talk, but Spencer had been repairing broken human bodies all morning, and

Grant had spent most of the afternoon on the phone.

Besides, Spencer didn't know what to say. He wasn't a fan of one-night stands, but if Grant suggested it, he'd take the chance to lose himself in all that strength, to watch Grant's blue eyes darken to midnight, to feel those hands on his body.

Was it fair to wish for that? Didn't Grant deserve a partner who made time for him? Who didn't spend more time in a hospital than outside it?

"Here."

Spencer jumped. "What?" He'd been so spun into his thoughts he hadn't noticed Grant move. Now the man waggled an object in front of his face.

"Here. You look like you could do with a treat."

The deep purple of the wrapper registered first. Then the gold. And then Spencer had to bite his lip so he wouldn't squeal. "Patchwork! How did you know?" Patchwork chocolate bars were his pick-me-up of choice and this one was his favourite mix. White chocolate with almonds and honey. Dark chocolate with chilli and sea salt. And milk chocolate with coco nibs and raspberries, all arranged in a patchwork of squares. "Tell me," he demanded as he unwrapped the gift. "How did you know?"

"Your theatre nurse told me. I asked Luca to pick

up a box."

Spencer flushed. "That's really not your job."

"It is, though." Grant's smile made his heart beat faster. "Upset clients are harder to wrangle."

"I see. Enlightened self-interest. In that case, I'm sure you don't mind sharing." Spencer broke the bar in half—lengthways, so they both got a mix of flavours—and passed one piece back to Grant.

He took it. "Because upset bodyguards are harder to escape from?"

"I don't want to escape from you." The words were out before Spencer had the chance to stop them, so he ploughed on. "If I'd met you anywhere else—in the bakery, say—I might have asked you out, and you could have turned me down. It's a shame we lost out on that."

"I wouldn't have turned you down."

Spencer almost missed the whispered words. But then he savoured them, right along with the patchwork of chocolate goodness.

Something was wrong with Spencer's front door. The moment Grant turned into Spencer's driveway every hair on the back of his neck stood on end.

"Wait." He stopped Spencer with a hand on his arm.

"What is it?"

"My danger sense is screaming."

Spencer reached for the door handle. Withdrew his hand with an apologetic glance and wound down the window.

Petrol. So much, the light breeze hadn't dispersed the stink.

"Rainbows." Grant pointed to the coloured trail running up the steps. "That's what caught my eye."

"Someone spilled petrol on my doorstep?"

"On more than your doorstep, I think. The whole place reeks." He unbuckled his seatbelt. "Get out of the car and walk down the drive. There's no way of knowing how much they've spilled, and even a spark can set it off."

Spencer reached into the back for his briefcase and jacket, and Grant was grateful for a client trained to handle emergencies. Spencer didn't panic or ask unnecessary questions, even when the emergencies kept coming.

"I wish we *had* met at the bakery," Grant said as they jogged to the end of the drive. "I'd dearly love to answer a goofy pickup line."

"My pickup lines are not goofy."

Grant would never find out. Instead, he had to watch Spencer get hurt once more. He clapped the phone to his ear. "Hi Josh. It's Grant. I may have a firebomb. No, it's a client's house. We just got here. Drive stinks of petrol and there are patches of it on the front doorstep. Yeah, we're at the bottom of the drive. Didn't start up the car again. Okay." He rang off and turned to Spencer. "They'll be here in a few."

Spencer didn't answer. He stared at his home, shoulders tight and expression closed off.

Hurting, just as Grant had thought. And probably for all the wrong reasons. "If you hadn't hired us," he said, "the stalker would still have escalated. Only then, you'd have had nobody in your corner. As it is, Cap has eyes on your ex, and if he's responsible for this, it stops today."

Spencer turned. Met Grant's gaze. "You're following Carlo?"

"Yes. Cap didn't like his attitude when he talked to him." He shrugged. "Major mistake, pissing off Fritz. Which reminds me." He raised the phone again. "There's a trap at the doc's house. Possibly a firebomb," he said. "Any chance it was the ex?"

"If it was, we'll nail him to the fence. You two okay?"

"Fine. Waiting for the fire brigade. Petrol on the drive. We didn't go in."

"Sensible. Get the doc to grab some clothes if he can. Call me if he can't. We get the house ready for him."

"Mine," Grant said, hating the idea of being a hundred yards from Spencer, even if he was perfectly safe.

Fritz chuckled, but at least he kept his evil bastard tendencies under wraps. "We'll see that everything is ready. Talk later."

Spencer had returned to the stiff-shouldered, blank-faced appraisal of his house. Grant wanted to pull him into a hug, reassure him they'd sort this out and that none of it was his fault.

Between sirens and flashing blue lights, he didn't get the chance.

CHAPTER SIX

Spencer sat up straight when Grant pulled into the drive of Knightdale Court. "Why are we stopping at your office? Is there something we need?"

"Ah—no. Knightdale Court isn't just our company HQ. I live here."

"You live at Knightdale Court?"

"We all do." The mews lay deserted when Grant parked the Range Rover in his accustomed spot, letting him know Fritz, Luca, and Rylan were working. Grant hoped they got to the bottom of this mess. "The place belonged to Cap's aunt," Grant said. "She left it to him. It's so utterly perfect for what we needed, we divided it between us."

"Divided it how? You each own part of the building?"

"Yes, exactly that. Each corner is a three-storey

townhouse. The company offices take up the centre, and we have training space, garages, and two guest houses in the mews."

"Guest houses? For clients?"

"Or contractors."

"And that's where I'll be staying?"

"No. I don't want you out of my sight until that stalker's caught." He glanced across the centre console and saw a tiny smile on Spencer's face. "You're staying with me."

"Right." Spencer craned his neck to peek through the brick arch dividing the mews from the garden. "You can see the lake from here."

"I know. I'd suggest we grab a bottle of wine and take a boat out, but—"

"Not while the stalker is still after me? Fine. I'll bookmark it for later." Spencer sounded resigned. He lifted his jacket and briefcase from the backseat and followed Grant into the house.

Grant would have preferred it had Spencer complained or argued or thrown a tantrum. He was too accepting for someone who'd had his life threatened three times in as many days and had almost had his home destroyed.

"I'm sorry about the boat trip," he said as he led

Spencer into his living room. "I promise we'll get to that. Right now it's just too…"

Spencer's touch on his arm stopped him in his tracks. The chocolate gaze was deep and earnest. "Don't apologise. Please."

"I really feel I should. You brought us a problem and—so far—we've only made it worse."

"Mr Bronnley warned me that might happen, and I went ahead with hiring you, anyway. If you must blame someone—"

"No blame. We will sort this out. For now, make yourself at home. What can I get you? Beer? Wine? Something stronger? Is there anything you want?"

"For you to bend me over the back of the couch?"

Grant's breath stopped. Of all the requests, that one hadn't even crossed his mind. Now he couldn't picture anything else. "You want that?" he grated out.

"Been thinking about it all the way here," Spencer smirked, as if he knew how his words affected Grant.

Grant struggled to string two coherent thoughts together. He reminded himself Spencer was a client, and under enough stress to affect his decision-making.

It was no use.

He hauled Spencer against his body for a rough kiss that left them both weak-kneed.

Even a brief interruption to gulp in oxygen didn't calm Grant down. He felt as out of control as a schoolboy and seeing Spencer with his pupils blown and an impressive bulge in his trousers only added fuel to the fire.

Grant dove back in, matching Spencer's ferocity, and grinding against him as they kissed. "Are you fucking sure?" he demanded before he did anything they'd both regret.

Spencer held his gaze. "You can't imagine how sure I am. I need normal. Just for tonight, if that's all you have. But give me fucking normal, okay?"

"And normal is you, bent over the back of the couch. Got it."

It took a while before they got to that part. Kissing each other stupid was more important.

Spencer paid no attention to Grant's home, and Grant spared only a passing thought for the fact he'd never brought a lover to his place. The mesh of lips and tongues demanded his attention and left little room for anything else. At one point, Grant thought he heard the ping and clatter of buttons, but the impression faded with the next touch of Spencer's hands. When he finally found himself bending Spencer over the back of the couch, he had no idea how they'd got there.

Spencer, with his chinos around his ankles and his arse on display, was an image worthy of a wet dream. Grant kneaded the cheeks and slipped his thumbs into the crack to tease Spencer's hole, making Spencer moan. He wanted to fuck that sweet arse until they both screamed.

And he could.

Spencer was right here. Safe, and sound, and horny as hell.

"Tell me you want it," he ordered.

"Do I have to? Is the visual in any way ambiguous?"

Little shit was taunting him. Well … two could play that game.

Grant draped himself over Spencer's back and nuzzled his stubbled cheek into Spencer's neck. He felt the wave of shivers passing through Spencer, and loved the way Spencer gripped the sofa cushions until his knuckles turned white.

"Get on with it."

"Impatient." Grant ground his hard-on into Spencer's crease, teasing him. "You deserve a proper seeing to. Not a half-arsed rush job."

"You fucking talk too much." Spencer twisted, working his hand between them to unzip Grant's jeans.

Grant wasn't having it. Keeping Spencer on the edge became a cherished goal. He grabbed Spencer's wrists and pinned them to the cushions. "Keep your hands to yourself. You take what I'll give you when I'm ready to give it to you." He sucked Spencer's earlobe between his lips and bit down, making Spencer jerk and moan.

Oh, really?

He unzipped himself one-handed while caressing Spencer's arse. A string of condoms and a bottle of lube balanced on the arm of the couch, and while Grant had no idea when they'd stopped grappling long enough to find provisions, he didn't hesitate to use them.

Spencer groaned and stuck his arse out when Grant pushed a finger inside. "More. Give me more."

"You are an impatient little shit. I don't want to hurt you." Grant admired the way Spencer's arse swallowed his finger. That was hot. Though not as arousing as the little whimpers he drew from Spencer's throat when he moved the digit in and out. He added a second finger, and Spencer undulated and whined in response.

Grant grabbed hold of Spencer's head and bent to kiss him, hard and messy, while he worked to get

Spencer ready. There was no doubt Spencer wanted fucking, and Grant couldn't wait any longer.

He smoothed on a condom, slicked himself, and then guided his cock to Spencer's entrance.

"Don't fucking make me wait!"

Grant wasn't *that* evil. He rocked against Spencer and watched with rapt attention as Spencer's body swallowed him up.

Spencer moaned, long and soft. His hands clutched at the sofa, and he didn't hold still. He pushed himself against Grant's intruding cock until Grant almost backed away, afraid to cause pain.

Then Spencer's muscles gave and Grant slid home.

It felt as if an inferno engulfed him. Hot. Tight. And oh, so fucking good.

Grant leaned over Spencer and found his mouth again, kissing him with near desperation. And Spencer, pinned and filled, allowed it. Let himself be kissed and mauled. Grant felt it when Spencer gave himself over, went loose and pliant. That was when he moved.

"You're so fucking gorgeous." Grant fucked into Spencer in short, sharp jabs. Threw in a few longer, slower thrusts to change things up. Hit Spencer's prostate until the doctor howled and found himself on the edge much sooner than he'd expected.

Spencer wasn't in much better shape. When Grant reached for Spencer's cock, he found him hard and leaking, straining into Grant's fist.

It broke his brain.

He let his inner caveman off the leash and rutted against Spencer, thrust after thrust after thrust, sliding his fist over Spencer's cock in counterpoint.

Spencer keened and clenched around Grant. He arched over the couch, chasing his orgasm, until Grant read his frustration in the movements of his body and heard it in his cries.

He slapped Spencer's arse. Hard.

It was enough to send Spencer over the edge and have Grant follow right after.

The room was silent for a long time, while they both returned to earth.

"Fuck, that was good." Spencer hung like a wet rag over the back of the couch. "Can we do it again?"

Grant pulled out. "You're great for my ego." He admired the handprint on Spencer's right arse cheek, the finger-shaped bruises on his hips. The doc wouldn't forget Grant for at least a few days. "I'm all for round two, but how about a shower first?"

"That sounds heavenly." Spencer pushed himself upright and sent a sated little smile Grant's way. "Don't you wish all disaster days would end like this?"

"How did you know what my favourite wine is?" Spencer asked when he saw the bottle Grant held. After making use of Grant's oversized shower, Spencer had needed a drink more than he needed dinner. He hadn't expected Grant to bring a bottle of Azevedo to bed with him.

"I'm in the business of knowing things. Or finding them out." Grant handed Spencer the glasses. "Though I can't claim points for this one. Fritz noticed your wine rack and the wine you had the most of."

The simple explanation didn't lessen Spencer's unease. He was attracted to Grant. Loved talking to him, cooking for him, being the focus of Grant's attention. And if their earlier encounter was anything to go by, their chemistry was combustible. But how safe was a man who'd sniffed out most of Spencer's likes and dislikes after only a couple of days? Who had taken Spencer to his own home and stocked Spencer's favourite wine?

"I've never had a client in my home. We have a guesthouse in the grounds for that," Grant said, proving he could mind-read, too. "I didn't want to leave you alone after the crap that happened this week, and I wanted you to feel comfortable. Which is why I made Fritz get me sandwich fixings from Boltoni's, and triple choc and sea salt deep dish cookies."

"Topflight customer service, that. Nothing but the best."

"You know it."

They clinked glasses. Spencer took a sip, leaned into the pillows, and took stock. His life was a mess, his emotions all over the place. Fritz had warned him the stalker might step up the attacks when Spencer showed he had protection. Spencer had accepted that risk. He hadn't thought he'd put Grant in the line of fire.

"Penny for them?"

Grant. Noticing his preoccupation, of course. He'd been told that he was closed off and difficult to read, yet Grant read him just fine. Spencer had never clicked so fast with anyone, and it amazed and scared him at once. He found a smile and turned his head, meeting Grant's deep blue gaze. "Just … rummaging around in my head."

"Bad habit, that."

"You think so?"

"With your stressful job? Yeah."

When Spencer looked past the broad shoulders and trim waist, when he ignored the blue eyes, and the enticing scruff, he saw scars. Thin, almost invisible ones. Larger tears and rips that had left silvery lines. And those that jumped right out at him. "You're telling me your job wasn't stressful?"

Grant laughed. "It was plenty stressful. That's why I don't rummage around in my head. I'm one of the lucky ones, I suppose. I take each op as it happens, review it when it's over, draw my conclusions, and move on."

"Bullshit." That came out with more force than Spencer had intended, and he held out a hand, almost in apology. "You compartmentalise well," he said, "but you dream like the rest of us."

Grant's body relaxed at the use of '*us*', and Spencer knew that admitting his fears had been the right way to go. It wasn't far enough, though. Sex with Grant had done much to quench Spencer's fury, but it hadn't sated the wanting. The curl of heat in his belly left him twitchy. His skin felt too tight, and he wanted his hands back on Grant.

When Grant slid deeper into the cushions, he swung a leg over Grant's, and planted himself squarely in Grant's lap.

Grant settled his hands on Spencer's hips. Otherwise, though, he didn't move, leaving Spencer to do as he pleased.

Spencer loved it. He'd wanted to touch and tease, and a bare skinned Grant was a sight to behold. Spencer felt like a little boy in a sweet shop.

"A genuine, honest-to-God eight pack!" He trailed his fingers over Grant's rippling muscles. "Even in my line of work, I don't see too many of these."

His line of work ensured he could name every muscle and tendon, but Grant arching into his touch wasn't an incentive to prove it. Cataloguing scars didn't make the list either. Instead, Spencer rocked on Grant's lap, felt Grant harden beneath him, and then leaned forward for a kiss that held all of his need.

He knew what he wanted, and that was Grant buried back in his arse. Saying so while Grant was looking at him, though…

Grant saved him the trouble. He curled upward, demanding more of Spencer's mouth, more of his wandering hands, more of the teasing weight on his crotch.

Spencer shivered under the onslaught. He retained enough awareness to reach for condom and lube, to get Grant covered and slick. Then he lost himself in heat and touch. In the stretch and burn. In zings of pleasure and—finally—in bliss.

His phone woke Grant from an erotic dream of fooling around with Spencer on a boat. He wanted to roll over and go right back to that. He reached for his phone instead. "Yeah?"

"Breakfast in the hall in an hour. Be there."

Grant pushed himself upright and groaned when he caught sight of the clock on his bedside table. After the days they'd had, quarter to six was too damned early! Worse, the call had woken Spencer.

"Problem?"

Grant shook his head. "Team breakfast."

"Oh, okay." Spencer let his lids drift down once more.

"You don't understand." Grant wrapped himself around Spencer and peppered his hair and forehead with kisses. "You need to be there, too."

"Why?"

"We need to review the evidence and make plans to end this."

Spencer didn't move. He lifted his face and let Grant kiss him stupid. It was scary—and perfect—how much Grant loved this.

When the grandfather clock in Grant's living room boomed a reminder of time passing, Spencer finally sat up. "Shame we can't delay the start of the day any longer. I need a shower. And can I borrow a shirt?"

CHAPTER SEVEN

The knowing looks he attracted when he arrived for breakfast wearing Grant's shirt didn't bother Spencer. The condition of the man on the other side of the table most certainly did.

"How long since the accident?" he barked, crossing the room in long, urgent strides.

Grant was right behind him. "Rylan? You're hurt?"

"Of course he's hurt. Look at him. Listen to his breathing. Do you have a headache? Chest pains?" That Grant's friend stared at him as if he spoke a foreign language was another clue Spencer didn't need. "Can you tell me what happened?"

Rylan turned his head and met Grant's gaze. "This is your doctor?"

Spencer scowled, then started palpitating Rylan's skull and neck. "I'm a surgeon," he said as he worked.

"Let's save the proper introductions for later. Tell me when this happened and how?"

"Nothing happened."

"Of course not. You always struggle for breath like a landed fish. Take that shirt off." Despite the sharp tone, his hands were gentle as he lifted the T-shirt over Rylan's head. Rylan neither helped nor hindered, and within seconds, the reason was clear. Purple and blue splotches mottled the right side of his chest.

"When and how?" Spencer asked again, checking each rib.

"Last night. No. One before."

"How?"

"I ... A target tried to commit suicide."

"You said he tried to drive into a river. Did you step in front of his car?" Grant sounded so horrified, Spencer didn't bother asking for confirmation. The extent of the bruising bore him out.

"Nothing's broken," Rylan objected. "I know what broken ribs feel like."

"Is there a problem?" Fritz joined them, carrying a pot of coffee. "Fucking hell!"

"Quite." Spencer raised his head and met Fritz's gaze. "He needs a hospital. Stat."

Grant wanted to argue. Rylan wanted to argue. Fritz actually tried. Spencer didn't listen to a single one of them. He stayed beside Rylan in the back of the car while Fritz drove, eyes on his patient and the phone to his ear, organising a welcoming committee. Within moments of Fritz pulling up outside the Accident & Emergency department, a team of nurses whisked Rylan inside. Spencer disappeared with them, and Grant wanted to swear. His doctor had gone to save Rylan's life, but he was still a stalker's target and this place wasn't safe.

"Spencer Corel's quite something." Fritz had conjured coffee and pressed a paper cup into Grant's hands. "Don't let him escape."

"What? Who?"

A sharp slap to the back of his head almost made him spill the coffee. "Fucking keep up. That man is worth holding onto, you hear me?"

Grant scowled. He would not discuss his sex life or the state of his emotions standing in the middle of a busy A&E department. Not even if Fritz insisted. "What happened to Ry?"

"You heard. His target tried to top himself."

"He told me that bit. If he stopped the car with his body, why the fuck didn't he go to the hospital?"

"Your guess is as good as mine. Actually, since it's Rylan, your guess will be better. He came home looking rough, but he said he was fine and I believed him. He's not as averse to hospital treatments as you and Luca."

"True. Only he wasn't as fine as he thought."

"Judging by Spencer's reaction…"

"Fuck!" Grant wanted to pace. Hit something. Shake Rylan until the idiot's teeth rattled. And do it while keeping watch over Spencer. "I hate waiting," he ground out.

"Don't we all?" Fritz pulled him to a seat beside the doors Spencer and Rylan had disappeared through. "Your man is pretty decisive. Let's hope he'll get matters sorted without a lengthy wait."

A nurse from his theatre team handed him a mug of coffee. Spencer sipped the steaming, sugar-laced liquid while scrutinising Rylan's scans over the radiographer's shoulder.

"No broken ribs. No pneumothorax. He was right

about that," the woman said.

"But a sea of contusion."

"Quite." She traced the edges of the affected area. "The bruising is extensive enough to make him an ARDS risk. How long ago did this happen?"

"Thirty-six hours. You think it's still spreading?"

"Possibly. I suggest we repeat the scan in twelve hours and see."

"Good call. He's on supplemental oxygen and already breathing more easily. I'll get him set up with fluids and talk to his friends." He returned the way he'd come, issuing orders and instructions for Rylan's care before heading to the waiting area.

Grant and Fritz had staked out a corner. They sat close together, not needing words to comfort each other, and Spencer was glad to see the bond between them, even if their closeness made him feel like an intruder.

He reached for the curtain when a third man joined Grant and Fritz. He appeared younger, but seeing how Grant and Fritz hugged him, he had to be Luca, the fourth member of White Knight Security.

"How is Ry?" he asked the moment Fritz let him go. "What's wrong with him? When he came home, he only mentioned bruises."

"No idea. Spencer went spare the moment he caught sight of Ry. They're working on him." Fritz pulled Luca to the side. "Now tell me what you found. And sit down! You're blocking the aisle."

Luca sat. "I don't think Carlo Sigismund is the stalker. But he has this new guy and that one's a whack job. According to my witnesses, he's the one who believes that Carlo wants to get back with your doctor, Grant. He said he's tried to—and I quote—*scare Spencer off*, only it hadn't worked. I have the feeling he's going to attempt something else."

The words sent a chill into Spencer's blood. Carlo's lover was sending poisoned chocolates, damaging his brakes, and dowsing his home with petrol? Because he thought Carlo wanted Spencer back?

"Give me a name." Grant sounded as if he'd been chewing ground glass. The tiny proof that Grant cared warmed Spencer. He wanted to comfort Grant, tell the three of them that Rylan's condition was improving, but he stayed still. He wanted a name, too.

"Luca?" Fritz already had his phone out.

Luca hesitated. "The police won't act on my gut feelings. We need actual evidence."

"And while we gather that, Spencer remains in danger. Luca, I want a chance with Spencer. I want to see if we can build something together. But I can't ask while he pays me to watch over him."

Spencer couldn't breathe. He wanted to step out from behind the curtain and claim Grant for himself. But Grant had a point, and Spencer had to leave him to make his own choices. Besides, while Luca sat gaping at Grant, Fritz was pushing the conversation where Spencer wanted it.

"I won't call the police without data," he said. "But Grant is right, Luca. We need to find this man."

"His name is Matthias Sharp. He's a procurement manager for this hospital."

The A&E, a place Spencer knew like the back of his hand, winked out of existence. For half a dozen heartbeats, he stood unmoving. Then he spun and sprinted down the corridor to the lift.

He'd wished for this. Now here was his chance to end this whole mess.

Procurement had offices on the third floor, grouped around a small reception area. The reception desk stood empty when Spencer arrived, but the offices bore name tags, and that was all he needed.

He raised his hand to knock on Sharp's door and hesitated. He only knew Matthias Sharp by sight. Had never exchanged a single word with him. What was he going to say? *You're welcome to Carlo. Now stop trying to kill me?*

Spencer gained a better appreciation for Luca's dilemma. Then he knocked anyway.

No invitation to enter came.

He turned the handle.

The door opened on an empty room. Had Sharp stepped out for a coffee? Should Spencer wait wait? If Sharp came back and found him here, he'd have surprise on his side.

Before he had the chance to close the door, something heavy hit the back of his head.

CHAPTER EIGHT

Grant was no stranger to A&E department waiting rooms. He knew that while triage and treatment rooms were frantic, time in the waiting area ran in fits and starts. It felt as if hours had passed since Spencer had whisked Rylan out of sight, yet his watch told him they'd been here for two.

Which was still too long to be left without news. Even in a busy A&E.

Suddenly antsy, he rose and peered into the corridor leading to the treatment rooms. Nurses and orderlies passed back and forth, and when Grant spotted a face he recognised, he called out.

"Do you have any news about Rylan?"

The nurse joined them in the waiting area. "They're just settling him now. You know he had his scan, yes? Mr Corel said he was going to update you.

Didn't he speak to you?"

"Not since we came in."

"That's odd. Someone must have grabbed him on the way. Let me see where he is."

She disappeared down the corridor while Grant mulled that over. Spencer knew they'd worry about Ry. He wouldn't attend a fresh case without at least sending someone along to tell them how he was.

"Ry's had a scan, and the nurse said Spencer was coming to talk to us," he said, rejoining Cap and Luca.

"He hasn't."

"I know." A feeling of dread unfurled in Grant's gut. "That's not like him. He'd have come as he'd promised or sent someone. What if Sharp cornered him?"

"We need to find Matthias Sharp." Cap stood, ready to hunt the man down.

"You don't think—"

Grant met Luca's troubled gaze. "What?"

"Could he have heard us discussing Matthias Sharp?" A wave of his hand encompassed the waiting room. "There's not a lot of privacy here, and those curtains—" He pointed at the cheerful check drape separating the treatment rooms from the waiting area. "They don't stop sound."

Grant couldn't breathe. Of course Spencer had

heard! And he'd want to settle the matter himself! "Bloody hell! He's gone after the bastard!"

"Is that something he'd do?"

"He felt guilty that hiring us put me in the line of fire. Of course, he'd try to fix this himself! We have to find him."

"We will. See? Fritz is already on it." Luca pointed to where Fritz stood by the reception desk.

Despite the hubbub in the waiting area, Fritz's voice reached them loud and clear. "I'm looking for Mr Matthias Sharp from Procurement. Can you direct me to his office?"

Whack job about covers it. Spencer's first thought on coming to wasn't a comforting one. It wasn't even funny. He'd dealt with his share of spaced-out, drunk, or aggressive patients, but none of them had ever taken a two-by-four to his head. Or tied him to a chair.

Spencer pried his eyes open—and closed them again in a hurry when the room spun. Nausea boiled in his gut, and he breathed through the need to throw up. *Possible concussion. Fabulous.*

"He's mine. He's always been mine. Even when

you stole him from me. He's mine."

The words ran together in a sibilant whisper, a hiss like a fishing line playing out and difficult to parse. Once the meaning behind them registered, though, Spencer couldn't unhear them.

"You're welcome to Carlo." He spoke slowly. Breathed through the nausea. Started over. "Carlo and I don't suit. We broke up seven months ago and haven't spoken since. If he's with you, he's yours."

"That's what you think!"

Sharp grabbed Spencer's hair and yanked his head back. The motion set the room spinning.

Spencer screwed his eyes shut.

He mustn't pass out. He was alone in a room with a confused, aggressive man.

He focussed on the pain in his head and the burn in his shoulders, then swallowed bile and gasped at the sting.

"He talks about you." Sharp had taken up his muttering again. "Tells me how perfect you are. How much I'm lacking. Always comparing. Always. He never did that before. Only once you'd stolen him from me. Why did you have to steal him from me?"

The wail made Spencer's ears ring and dialled the pain in his head up to eleven. The behaviour his captor described meshed with his own memories. Carlo had loved to find fault. He found pleasure in undermining someone's confidence. In making them feel lesser and worthless. Spencer had resisted the manipulation and had eventually thrown Carlo out. Matthias Sharp hadn't been so lucky.

He cudgelled his brain for the right words to penetrate the man's delusion. Words that brought him back to the present and made him realise what he was doing. But with his head pounding like a drum and the room spinning every time he opened his eyes…

"I'm going to kill you. That will stop you interfering."

"I have never interfered." Spencer knew he'd made a mistake. He'd come up here to talk sense into Matthias Sharp, to protect Grant, who already carried more scars than any man should collect in a lifetime.

It had been a noble gesture. And a stupid one. Because Sharp was clearly deranged. And since nobody knew he was here, nobody would come to his aid.

"You won't take him from me. You'll be dead, and he'll be mine."

Grant pressed his ear to Matthias Sharp's office door. "He's lost the plot," he whispered, loud enough for Fritz and Luca to hear.

"Spencer?"

"Nothing yet." Sharp's threats made Grant want to storm inside, but he had to know where Spencer was.

"Carlo is yours." Spencer was using his doctor voice—low and calm—trying to talk sense into someone who was beyond reach. "I don't love Carlo Sigismund. I love a man called Grant. Carlo is yours."

"He will be. Once you're dead."

Grant straightened. "Sharp's off his rocker, threatening to kill Spencer," he whispered. "Spencer's to our right. He's conscious."

They took up positions.

"Luca and I take Sharp. You protect Spencer."

"Done."

They shared a look, then Fritz nodded. "Go."

Sharp hadn't even locked the door. And while he wielded a knife, he was too far away to reach Spencer before Fritz tackled him to the floor.

Grant made a beeline for the doc, assessing his condition as he went. Spencer was conscious, his arms tied to the chair, and blood staining the neck of his scrubs.

"Are you hurt?"

"Don't yell," Spencer mumbled. "I may have a concussion. I'm about to—" He heaved once, twice, then screwed his eyes shut and just breathed.

Grant cut the bindings, then pulled Spencer into his arms. Relief almost buckled his knees when he held the warm, familiar weight and felt Spencer's heart beat against his. They'd only known each other a few days, but Grant had gone and fallen for the man and never realised it. Just as he hadn't realised that love came laced with fear.

He'd forever be afraid of someone taking Spencer from him. Or of Spencer going off on stupid-fool errands of his own. "What the fuck were you thinking?" he demanded, clutching Spencer as if he needed something to keep himself upright. "What the fuck was that?"

"I thought I could reason with him," Spencer said. "Explain that Carlo meant nothing to me."

"You're a fucking doctor. You know better. Going off without backup is stupid and irresponsible!"

"I said DON'T YELL!" Spencer took a step back, clearly not realising he was the one doing the yelling. "I'm stupid? You're one to talk. You get paid to walk into dangerous situations."

"We're also trained to deal with situations like that."

"Yeah? Is that why you're covered in scars? Training? Why Rylan has a massive lung contusion and could barely breathe when I saw him? How the fuck can you claim to take care of clients when you don't even take care of your best friend?"

They stared at each other across three feet of distance that felt as wide as an ocean.

Grant was the first to look away.

He hadn't meant to shout at Spencer, and now he didn't know how to take back his words. He wasn't even sure he wanted to. Spencer *had* been reckless and—

"Grant! Give me a hand."

Fritz's call felt like a lifeline, guiding him through the mess he'd made. He crossed the room to Fritz's side and helped him restrain a sullen Matthias Sharp. "What are we doing with him?"

"Nothing. Luca's called hospital security. It's their pigeon."

Grant opened his mouth to answer, when the sound of many voices washed into the room. Security arrived, along with nurses in scrubs. Fritz shoved Mattias Sharp into their arms and pulled Grant out of the way to where Luca stood, observing the melee.

When Grant turned back to the room, Spencer had vanished.

CHAPTER NINE

Spencer scrubbed the floor for the third time in as many days. Then he steeped lemon slices and rosemary sprigs in hot water and used the solution to wipe down walls, cupboards, and kitchen worktops, ignoring the ache behind his eyes and the snatches of vertigo that had him stumbling whenever he moved his head too quickly. His home was immaculate, but—to Spencer's senses—the smell of petrol still tainted the air. He just couldn't get it out of his nose.

His house also felt emptier than it ever had before.

His bed was bigger and colder—even though Grant had never slept in it.

Even his dining table gave the impression it had grown overnight.

He'd noticed none of those shortcomings before he'd met Grant, nor had they been apparent while

Grant had been in his home. It was his absence that had brought the defects into focus. That had made Spencer realise what he was missing.

Couldn't the damned man at least text him?

But why should he, seeing he'd raced to Spencer's rescue, only for Spencer to yell at him?

Besides, they'd both told other people how they felt, but they'd never told each other. Spencer couldn't stop hearing the words. Grant's to Fritz and Luca. His own to the man who'd threatened to kill him. Somewhere along the line, those words should have connected, and they hadn't. And now Spencer felt lost and alone, and he didn't care for the feeling.

His phone chimed, and he was glad for the interruption. "Cath, hi."

"Hi, Spencer. How's the head?" His lead theatre nurse had the best bedside manner of anyone he knew.

"Still grumbling." He'd have welcomed the distraction of a busy A&E department, but he wouldn't put patients' lives in danger. "I can come back for rounds and paperwork if you need me."

"We'll survive until you're fit. I just called to say that Dr Grimlen has moved Matthias Sharp to psych assessment. Oh, and Susie has released Rylan Jeffers."

"That was quick."

"The contusion's healing well. She thinks it's due to you dragging him in here when you did. If he'd waited a few days longer, he'd have ended up on a ventilator. His friends have picked him up. They asked after you."

Her words triggered such a wave of longing that Spencer ended the call on autopilot. All his thoughts were of Grant and the hours he'd spent at Knightdale Court.

And he knew, beyond any doubt, he couldn't let things end this way.

"Come on, fess up! What's got you so miserable?" Rylan made himself comfortable on Grant's sofa and accepted the mug of coffee Grant handed him. "You bounced around like peas on a hot shovel while we were in the hospital, and now you look like you want to crawl into a bottle. Level with me, bro."

"Your similes are horrible."

"They got my point across. Where's your doctor?" As usual, Rylan was uncomfortably perceptive.

"That's exactly the problem," Grant muttered. "I shouted at him. He shouted right back. And I haven't seen him since."

"I heard he had a mild concussion. They sent him home to rest his head."

Grant winced. He'd regretted shouting at Spencer as much as he'd regretted leaving the hospital in a huff without checking on the man. He'd been shaking with a baffling mix of adrenaline, fear, and relief and hadn't realised what he was doing until he'd reached the carpark. And then he hadn't known how to go back.

"Are you telling me you haven't called him? Or even texted? Grant, really?"

"I was mad at him for risking his life. I mean, who does that? Who walks right up to their stalker and tries to talk to them?"

"A person who runs on compassion, obviously."

Rylan struggled a little more upright, and Grant shoved another cushion behind his back. The damage to his lungs needed more time to heal, and the doctor had given them strict instructions about how to keep Rylan comfortable.

"What did you say to him?"

Grant buried his face in his hands. "I don't know. Really. I was mad. Just blurted shit out. Didn't mean any of it."

"Are you sure? You're a bossy bastard who wants to have his way."

"I wanted to protect him. Keep him safe."

"I get that. But he's a trauma surgeon. He deals with emergencies all day long. He makes life and death decisions. Sometimes, that means he has to risk himself. You can't take that away from him."

"I know." He knew Rylan watched him, as intent as a cat before a mouse hole, and did his best not to squirm.

"You don't have a clue," Rylan said. "Let me spell it out. This is your fuck-up. If you want him back, you need to fix this. Call him. Go see him. Write him a fucking note. Just don't assume he's clairvoyant." Without waiting for an answer, Rylan picked up the remote control and turned to a documentary, leaving Grant to ponder his words.

Who the fuck was at the door? Grant felt as if he'd just fallen asleep when the doorbell jerked him awake. He shuffled into the hallway, trying to remember if he'd ordered anything. Most of the delivery services in the area dropped parcels off at the front entrance. Maybe they had a new driver.

He yanked the door open.

Spencer Corel, in tight jeans and a dark brown T-shirt that matched his eyes and set off the gold in his hair, stood on his porch holding a cake tin. A tiny, careful smile curved his lips. "Fritz told me you were home. I want to talk to you, and I thought the conversation might be easier with cake. It's apple with cinnamon cream."

Grant's mouth watered at the thought of apples and cinnamon. It watered even more at the idea of Spencer wanting to share a treat with him, when he hadn't come up with any reunion strategies of his own. Rylan's words had kept him awake until the early hours, and now he felt off kilter. He was present enough to hold the door wide for Spencer and to find the on-switch for the coffeemaker.

"I should apologise," he said.

"You should, yes. Question is, do you want to?"

Grant stilled, his back to Spencer. "Of course I want to. I don't really remember what I said, and I didn't mean any of it."

"That's good to know." Spencer wrapped his arms around Grant's middle and leaned his cheek against Grant's back. "Because neither did I. Not the bits I yelled at you. That was … blowing off steam. Emotional overspill."

Grant sagged with relief. He clasped Spencer's hands where they rested on his stomach and held tight. "That's exactly what it was. Fear and relief and adrenaline."

"A highly combustible mix."

The kitchen grew silent except for the gurgling of the coffeemaker. Grant watched it drip coffee into the jug and soaked up Spencer's warmth and solidity. When the coffee was done brewing, he loosened Spencer's arms and reached for cups and plates.

Spencer cut the cake, stopping twice to stifle a yawn.

"Restless night?"

"You said it." Dark chocolate eyes met Grant's. "Do you know? At some point yesterday, I realised that I'd told Sharp I was in love with you, but that I'd never told you. It bothered me."

Grant couldn't stop the silly grin spreading over his face. Nor did he want to. "I told my friends I wanted to spend more time with you and try for something solid, but I never told you, either."

"I heard it, though. Overheard it, really."

"I heard you talking to Sharp, too."

Their laughter came like the tide, slow at first, but with a relentless power neither could withstand. They laughed until they were out of breath and tear tracks marred their faces. Kept chuckling even as they drank their cooling coffee and left the cake for later.

"Bed?" Grant held out a hand, and Spencer clasped it without hesitation.

"The best remedy for sleepless nights."

Grant's cock pushing into his arse was—in Spencer's opinion—the absolute best way to start a morning. And while he knew he didn't have to be quiet, restraining himself added an extra dimension to the sex.

Spencer buried his face in the pillow and revelled in Grant's warm weight draped over his back. The tight clutch of fingers on his hips. The lips and teeth on his nape and—most of all—that hot, heavy cock sliding in and out, stretching him and hitting every single hot spot he possessed.

He wanted to beg for faster and harder.

He also didn't.

They'd spent the previous day and night in bed, sleeping, making love, dozing, and talking. Long, meandering conversations about everything and nothing that had settled them both.

If Grant wanted to start the morning taking Spencer apart, bit by delicious bit, then Spencer was right here for it. He moaned when Grant found a sensitive spot, and pushed into every thrust, feeling himself careen closer and closer to the edge. His climax would be incandescent and keep him lit for the rest of the day. He was fine with that, too.

He tensed as Grant's thrusts grew erratic. And then they were falling. Tumbling over the edge in a tangle of limbs and kisses.

They'd barely caught their breaths when Grant's phone chimed.

"Team breakfast in an hour," Fritz ordered, loud enough for Spencer to hear. "Be there."

Grant dropped the phone onto the bedside table and rearranged the covers. "Are you up for team breakfast?" he asked.

Spencer wrapped both arms around him and nuzzled into his neck. "Sure. If you lend me a shirt."

Team breakfast turned into Sunday lunch, then turned into a lazy afternoon spent lounging by the lake.

Spencer checked on Rylan, who complained that Fritz had buried him under a mountain of paperwork and had forbidden him from lifting anything heavier than a coffee mug. He ate too much and listened to the others telling him off for being reckless. Eventually, he drifted down to the jetty, where he dangled his feet in the water, paying only scant attention to the insults and teasing flashing back and forth behind him.

He'd come to Knightdale Court in search of help and had liked the men he'd met. Comfortable alone, Spencer had few friends outside of the hospital and hadn't expected to be pulled into their circle, or to be comforted by the way they cared for each other and worked together towards a common goal. They were a family, and Spencer hadn't thought to be included.

He might have met and fallen for Grant at any other time. But seeing Grant interact with his family and having the others rallying around them both made him realise that this—Grant and family—was something he wanted.

"Are you okay?" Grant plopped down beside him. "They guys aren't putting you off, are they? We can be overwhelming en mass, but we mean well. Truly."

"Don't doubt it for a moment. It's a great setup you have here."

"We're close. We give each other room."

"And we're happy to make space for… significant others, say?"

Spencer twisted and stared up at Fritz, then down at the man's smart leather shoes. "How do you move so quietly?"

"It's a knack." Fritz grinned. "But please, I meant what I said. Grant has never acted like this over anyone. You mean the world to him, and we don't want to get in the way of that. We'll give you room to sort yourselves out."

"Will you shut up!"

Spencer didn't know how to answer. Not when Grant was attempting to toss Fritz off the jetty, while Luca and Rylan cheered and bet on the outcome of that fight. He took a sip from his beer and watched.

Maybe he and Grant could build something out of their mutual affection.

Maybe it wouldn't work out.

But Spencer thought it was worth a try.

NEXT: RYLAN'S STORY

Can Rylan find a partner who isn't overwhelmed by his protective nature and offers him a chance to fulfil an old, long-forgotten dream? Find out in the second book of the White Knight Security series.

"Come in, come in." Spencer Corel signed his name to the last report and slumped in his chair. He'd been on call for a day and a night and felt every one of those hours. Grant's appearance, while unexpected, was more than welcome. Especially since Grant hadn't come empty-handed. "Please tell me that's coffee or I won't make it home with my eyes still open."

"Oh, go me!" Grant fished a thermos flask from the bag and set it on the corner of Spencer's desk. "I brought a gallon of hot, sweet coffee. Also, cream horns and chocolate croissants. That should hold you for a while."

"Life saver. Why are you even awake at this hour?"

Grant shrugged, as if turning up in Spencer's office at four in the morning was normal. "I couldn't sleep without you there. Weird, eh?"

Spencer's smile softened at the admission. He'd moved into Grant's place four days ago. Being together hadn't yet become routine. It hadn't even reached the 'normal' stage. He washed down his yawn with a mouthful of coffee. "It's just new. And my first night shift since I moved into your house."

"*Our* house. If it was that bad a shift, maybe I should drive us home."

"It's been non-stop. Multi-vehicle on the M40—that was nasty. Then another on the A41." He pulled the box of pastries closer. "Plus the usual emergencies."

"Good thing I'm here, right?"

Spencer licked sweet cream from his upper lip. "Very good thing. I have one more patient to check before I can leave. Would you come with me when I do?"

"Of course." Grant sat up straight. "Is he trouble?"

"What? No. Not at all."

"Right. Then what's the reason you need my oh-so-charming company?"

"His injuries."

"Oh?"

"Impact trauma to head and torso. I've seen patterns like that before. Punishment beatings, you know?"

"Has he said anything?"

"He was unconscious when he arrived, but... I know him. Or rather, I know who he is."

"You do?"

"Kris Hillyard. He owns Gloss." He registered Grant's blank look and shrugged. "Nightclub in High Wycombe."

"And you think he's in trouble."

"With those injuries?"

Grant, co-owner of White Knight Security, put his phone to his ear. "Hi, Ry. Sorry to wake you. Can I pick your brain? Nightclub in High Wycombe, name of Gloss. Heard of it? Any issues you're aware of? Spencer has the owner on his ward. Badly beaten. Kris Hillyard, yes. That's the name. You know him?" He listened for a moment longer, and then his grin went feral. "Am I hearing interest there? Someone got under your armour. Really?" He held the phone away from his ear while he waited out the swearing. "Don't give me that. You pull that mind-reading crap on us all the time. The one time I do it to you—" Grant's voice took on a conciliatory note as he continued the conversation. "Don't break the laws of physics, Rylan. I'll watch over him until you get here. I promise, bro."

When he turned back to Spencer, he wore a wide, delighted smile. "Seems Rylan has had his eye on your patient for a while now. For not entirely professional reasons, I think. He's coming over."

Meet Jackie

Jackie Keswick was born behind the Iron Curtain with itchy feet, a bent for rocks, and a recurring dream of stepping off a bus in the middle of nowhere to go home. She's worked in a hospital and as the only girl with 52 men on an oil rig, spent a winter in Moscow and a summer in Iceland and finally settled in the country of her dreams with her dream team: a husband, a cat, a tandem, and a laptop.

Jackie writes a mix of suspense, action adventure, fantasy and history, loves stories with layers, plots with twists and characters with hidden depths. She adores friends to lovers stories, and tales of unexpected reunions, second chances, and men who write their own rules. She blogs about English history and food, has a thing for green eyes, and is a great believer in making up soundtracks for everything, including her characters and the cat.

And she still hasn't found the place where the bus stops.

To chat with Jackie about books, boys and food, join her in her Facebook readers group Jackie's Kitchen, or join her on Ream for bonus reads, snippets, and new stories.

JACKIE KESWICK